STARTERS

Shred it Skateboarding

Jaime Winters

🌳 Crabtree Publishing Company

www.crabtreebooks.com

SPORTS STARTERS

Created by Bobbie Kalman

Author
Jaime Winters

Project coordinator
Kathy Middleton

Editors
Molly Aloian
Kathryn White

Proofreader
Wendy Scavuzzo

Photo research
Melissa McClellan

Design
Tibor Choleva
Melissa McClellan

Production coordinator
Margaret Amy Salter

Prepress technician
Margaret Amy Salter

Print coordinator
Katherine Berti

Consultant
Max Dufour, X-games silver medalist,
2007 Silver best trick, Vert Pro-skater 1995-2007
Philip Klager

Special thanks to
Molly Klager

Illustrations
Leif Peng: page 11

Photographs
Shutterstock.com: © goldenangel (p 12); © Mark Stout Photography (p 14);
© gravity imaging (p 17); © Stephen Bonk (p 19); © Kim Reinick (p 24); © Sadi
Pekerol (p 25); © homydesign (p 26); Ahmad Faizal Yahya (back cover, p 27);
Charles Shapiro (p 31 bottom) / iStockphoto.com: © Daniel Brunner (front cover); ©
Christian Carroll (p 5 b) / fotolia: © Fred Sweet (toc page); © Lucky Dragon (p 11);
Fotolia XXIV (p 13 right); © auremar (p 16); © Galina Barskaya (p 31 middle) /
Thinkstock: © Comstock (icon, every page); © Getty Images (pp 7, 31); © Ingram
Publishing (pp 23, 31) / dreamstime.com: © Redbaron (titlepage); © Larisap (p 4); ©
Stephen Coburn (p 5 top); © Jirk4 (p 6 left); © Denis Radovanovic (p 10); ©
Arenacreative (p 13 left); © Gerry Boughan (p 15); © Willeecole (p 18); © Plaquon (p
20); © Ahmad Faizal Yahya (p 21 left); © Daniel Halfmann (p 21 right); © Chris
Johnson (pp 22); © Tom Ferris (p 29) / Corbis: Tony Donaldson (p 28) / ©
MMcClellan (p 6 right)
Created for Crabtree Publishing by BlueApple*Works*

Library and Archives Canada Cataloguing in Publication

Winters, Jaime
   Shred it skateboarding / Jaime Winters.

(Sports starters)
Includes index.
Issued also in electronic format.
ISBN 978-0-7787-3151-1 (bound).--ISBN 978-0-7787-3162-7 (pbk.)

   1. Skateboarding--Juvenile literature. I. Title.
II. Series: Sports starters (St. Catharines, Ont.)

GV859.8.W573 2012   j796.22   C2012-900874-5

Library of Congress Cataloging-in-Publication Data

Winters, Jaime.
   Shred it skateboarding / Jaime Winters.
      p. cm. -- (Sports starters)
   Includes index.
   ISBN 978-0-7787-3151-1 (reinforced library binding : alk. paper) --
ISBN 978-0-7787-3162-7 (pbk. : alk. paper) -- ISBN 978-1-4271-8849-6
(electronic pdf) -- ISBN 978-1-4271-9752-8 (electronic html)
   1. Skateboarding--Juvenile literature. I. Title.

GV859.8.W573 2012
796.22--dc23
                        2012004032

Crabtree Publishing Company

Printed in the U.S.A./032012/CJ20120215

www.crabtreebooks.com   1-800-387-7650

Published in Canada
Crabtree Publishing
616 Welland Ave.
St. Catharines, Ontario
L2M 5V6

Published in the United States
Crabtree Publishing
PMB 59051
350 Fifth Avenue, 59th Floor
New York, New York 10118

Published in the United Kingdom
Crabtree Publishing
Maritime House
Basin Road North, Hove
BN41 1WR

Published in Australia
Crabtree Publishing
3 Charles Street
Coburg North
VIC 3058

Contents

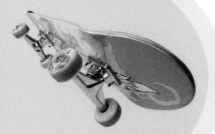

What is skateboarding?

Skateboarding is an individual sport that first caught on with surfers who wanted to surf on sidewalks the way they surfed on ocean waves. A skateboarder, or skater, rides a piece of equipment called a **skateboard**.

Skateboards are shaped like Band-Aids. The best quality skateboards are made of seven-ply Canadian maple wood. They have wheels made of polyurethane, a rubber-like material, for a smooth ride.

When the skateboard rolls forward, skateboarders stand on it and glide forward.

4

On the roll

Skaters ride to get around from place to place, and just to have fun. Skaters ride on sidewalks, large areas of concrete, and indoor and outdoor **skateparks**. With one foot on the board, they push against the ground with the other foot. This makes the skateboard roll forward. Then they bring the "pushing" foot onto the board to glide.

Skaters often ride their skateboards to get to school.

Experienced skateboarders can do many cool tricks.

Gear up

Apart from a skateboard, skaters do not need much equipment. Just a few pieces are essential. Comfortable running shoes with flat soles are a must to balance on the board. Wearing a helmet, elbow pads, and kneepads is also important to protect the body during falls on the ground.

Skate shoes have large, flat bottoms to better grip the board.

On the board

A skateboard has three main parts: a **deck**, wheels, and trucks. The deck is made of seven layers of wood that are glued together. Skaters stick **griptape**, which looks and feels like sandpaper, on the deck. Griptape helps their feet stay steady and grip the board.

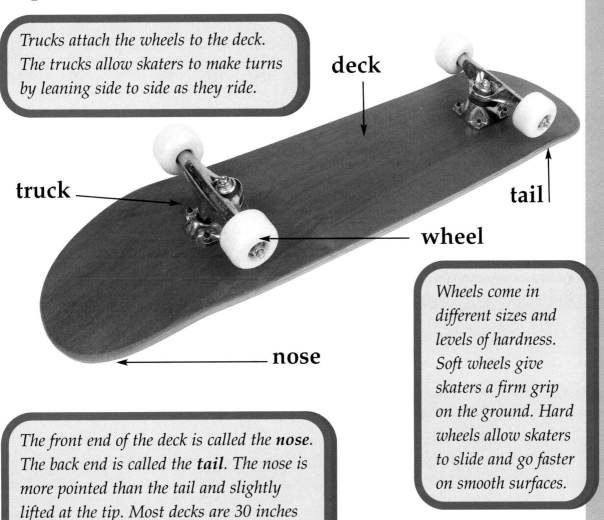

Trucks attach the wheels to the deck. The trucks allow skaters to make turns by leaning side to side as they ride.

deck

truck

tail

wheel

nose

Wheels come in different sizes and levels of hardness. Soft wheels give skaters a firm grip on the ground. Hard wheels allow skaters to slide and go faster on smooth surfaces.

*The front end of the deck is called the **nose**. The back end is called the **tail**. The nose is more pointed than the tail and slightly lifted at the tip. Most decks are 30 inches (76 cm) long and 8 inches (20 cm) wide.*

At the park

Many towns and cities have indoor and outdoor skateparks built for skateboarding. Most skateparks have **obstacles** for skaters to ride. Outdoor skateparks have obstacles, such as large bowls like swimming pools and **half-pipes** made of concrete. Indoor skateparks have obstacles, such as wooden **ramps** and banks.

Catching air

Skaters ride off the end of a ramp to launch themselves into the air. Riding up the sides of bowls and half-pipes allows skaters to get **big air**, the height to perform aerial tricks and moves.

half-pipe

bowl

A typical bowl skatepark.

full
pipe

bowl

The skatepark is made to allow skaters
to move quickly from one area to the next.
Bowl skateparks are made with concrete.

Get on board

Much the same as being right-handed or left-handed, skaters are **regular-footed** or **goofy-footed**. The names of these **stances** note the foot a skater leads with on the board. Regular-footed skaters ride with their left foot at the front of the board. Goofy-footed riders ride with their right foot at the front.

Regular or goofy

You can can tell if you are regular-footed or goofy-footed. Stand on a skateboard and try out each stance. Usually, one will feel more natural and comfortable than the other.

regular

Skaters practice pushing off and gliding until they have mastered the skill.

Pushing off

The first move skaters must master is pushing off. Pushing off gives the skateboard the **momentum**, or power, to move forward. Skaters push off by pushing against the ground with their back foot a few times. Then they can bring their back foot onto the board to glide.

The board stops here

Once skaters get the board rolling, they must learn to stop on the board. One way is to take the back foot off the board and drag it on the ground. This method is called **footbreaking**. Another way is to pull a **stop wheelie** by pressing the tail of the board into the ground to lift up the front wheels.

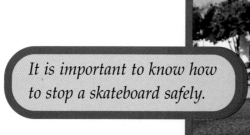

It is important to know how to stop a skateboard safely.

The easiest way to stop is to just jump off your skateboard.

Wearing pads will protect your knees and elbows.

If all else fails, bail

A third way to stop is to **bail**, or jump off the board. Jumping forward usually brings the skateboard to a stop and helps skaters clear the board safely.

Board-turning moves

Once skaters get comfortable starting and stopping, they practice making turns on the board.

Carve it

Carving allows skaters to turn easily by shifting their weight in either direction. With both feet pointing to one side of the board, skaters shift their weight **frontside** into their toes or **backside** into their heels. Depending on their stance, the board will turn either left or right.

Carving allows skaters to turn easily by shifting their weight.

Kick turns

When skaters do not have enough space or momentum to carve, they can do a kick turn by leaning in the direction they want to go and lifting their front foot slightly. This lifts the nose of the board off the ground, making it easier to move. Then they can pull or kick the board with their front foot in the direction they want to go.

Lifting the nose of the board off the ground makes it easier to turn either left or right.

The ollie

When skaters do **ollies**, they fly through the air with their skateboards stuck to the bottom of their feet. Not only does this look cool, but the ollie is a basic move of many other tricks. So it is one of the first tricks skaters must learn. It is also one of the most difficult.

The ollie is a basic move of many other tricks.

Popping off

For an ollie, the front foot goes behind the front truck. The back foot goes to the edge of the tail. The skater crouches down and stomps on the tail. This is called popping off because the nose pops up. The front foot slides up the board and the back foot lifts, causing the skater to sail through the air. The skater then lands on all four wheels.

This skater is practicing popping off.

Grinding and sliding

Once skaters can pop an ollie, they are ready to **grind** and **slide**. They can jump up onto obstacles and ride right over them.

Grind to go

When skaters grind, they travel along a handrail on the metal trucks of their skateboard. They do an ollie to jump up onto the handrail. Then they push down on the board with their feet to lock both trucks onto the rail and scoot over it. Skaters can grind on the front or back truck, lifting up the other end of the board.

When skaters grind, they travel along a rail on the metal trucks of their skateboard.

Sliding along benches or rails requires great skateboarding skills.

Slide to ride

Anything skaters can grind on, they can also **slide** on—gliding along a bench or bar on the bottom of their board. They ollie up onto the bench and then slide along it. Skaters can also do **noseslides** or **tailslides** on one end of the board as the other end hangs out over the edge of the bench or bar.

On the ramp

Riding on ramps takes skateboarders to the next level. Skateparks have mini ramps and tall ramps called **vert ramps**. "Vert" is short for the word "vertical," which means up and down. Most mini ramps are about four to five feet (1.2–1.5 meters) tall and 18 feet (5.5 m) wide. Vert ramps are between 10 to 13 feet (3–4 m), and they have vertical walls in the **transition** of one to two feet (30–60 cm) at the top.

Ramps usually have decks where skaters can wait and enter the ramp.

U shape to ride

Ramps have flat areas in the middle with curved areas called transitions on each side. Each transition leads into a vertical wall edged with steel tubing at the top. This edge is called the **coping**. Behind the coping is a deck where skaters can wait and enter the ramp.

Ramps are shaped like the letter "U."

Tricks for kicks

Skaters ride up and down the ramp. They build up speed to launch into the air at the top of the ramp to pull aerial spins, twists, turns, and grabs.

21

Half-pipe

Skaters also call vert ramps "half-pipes," because the ramps are shaped like half of a pipe. Half-pipes are made of wood or concrete and are usually at least 11 feet (3.4 m) tall.

Drop in

To enter the half-pipe, skaters drop in from the deck at the top. With the back edge of the skateboard on the coping, they stand with their back foot on the back edge. The front of the board hangs over the edge. Then skaters lean forward and bend their knees to roll down the ramp.

This skater is about to drop in from the deck at the top of a half-pipe.

Pump it up

Pumping helps skaters build up speed to get airborne. To pump, skaters ride back and forth on the half-pipe. They crouch down at the bottom of the half-pipe, then straighten their legs as they enter the curved areas and stand tall as they ride up the walls.

Skaters ride back and forth on the half-pipe to build up speed to get into the air.

Pulling tricks in thin air

Once skaters catch air, they can perform some eye-popping, jaw-dropping tricks in midair.

Handplant on the pipe

Some skaters fly high above the half-pipe to do a **handplant**. With their feet in the air, they grab the coping with one hand. They then grab their board with the other hand to hold it to their feet.

When doing a handplant, skateboarders grab the coping with one hand.

Skateboarders can do many different tricks when flying in the air.

Grab it

Soaring above the half-pipe, skaters often reach down to grab their board and hang on to it for as long as they can. To pull a **nose grab**, they grab the board's nose with their front hand. To do an **indy grab**, they grab the front side between the trucks with their back hand. In an **airwalk grab**, skaters hold the board's nose with their front hand and "walk on air" next to the board.

Competitions

Skateparks hold competitions for skaters of all levels, from beginner to pro. Pro skateboarders also compete at special events, such as the X Games, Tampa Pro, and DEW tour. Skaters compete in street and vert events.

Street events

Street events are held in a skatepark area that looks and feels like a real street. Riders perform a run of tricks, such as grinds, slides, and ollies, on a course of obstacles such as benches, stairs, curbs, and handrails. Judges give a score for each rider based on the degree of difficulty of tricks, style, execution, consistency, and originality.

This skateboarder is doing a trick high above a half-pipe.

Vert events

Riders compete in timed runs on the half-pipe. They ride up and down the half-pipe to perform tricks, such as grabs and spins. Judges give them points for execution, difficulty, and originality of tricks, as well as for their height and use of the ramp. Riders do three runs. The best score of the three becomes their final score, and the rider with the highest score wins.

Stars that rip

Some skaters reach the top level of the sport and become paid professionals. Skateboard and clothing companies **sponsor** pros.

Elissa Steamer smashes street

Elissa Steamer began skateboarding when she was only 13. In 1998, she won the Slam City Jam competition, the first woman's competition held by a World Cup Skateboarding event. Elissa has won several other competitions, including the X Games.

Elissa Steamer was the first female to star in a Tony Hawk video game.

Ryan Sheckler rocks

At 18 months old, Ryan Sheckler begged to ride his dad's skateboard! Ryan started skating when he was five and went pro at 13. In his first pro year, he rocked the skating world by winning five major events, including the X Games. When Ryan was seven, he got excited about doing **kickflips**. Now, his favorite trick is a **360 flip**.

Ryan Sheckler has been competing in street skating and park contests since 2002.

Shred it!

Hop on your board, push off, and ride. Skateboarding is a great way to have fun and stay fit. Skaters get a lot of exercise riding around local parks and skateparks. Skateboarding also helps develop balance and coordination. To perform tricks, a skater must stay steady on a moving board and change body positions.

Skatepark scene

Local skateparks usually welcome young members. Many skateparks offer lessons to help kids learn skateboarding skills and encourage kids to skate for the fun of it.

Always wear your helmet and other protective gear.

Skateboarding helps develop balance and coordination.

When you're ready for some skateboarding, be sure to ride in a safe place!

Glossary

Note: Boldfaced words that are defined in the text may not appear in the glossary.

360 flip A trick in which skaters kick the board in midair to flip it over while it spins around from tail to nose in a complete circle (360°)

backside The side of a skateboard that the rider's heels point toward

coping The metal tubing along the top edge of a half-pipe that skaters can grind and slide on

deck The wooden part of a skateboard that skaters stand on. Also, an area at the top of a half-pipe where skaters can wait and drop in

frontside The side of the skateboard that the rider's toes point toward

half-pipe A U-shaped ramp

kickflip A trick in which skaters kick the board in midair to flip it over so that it spins in a complete circle (360°)

nose The front end of a skateboard

ollie A trick in which skaters travel through midair as their skateboard sticks to their feet

sponsor A company that gives money to an athlete for training, clothes, equipment, etc.

vert ramps A form of half-pipe that transitions from a flat-bottom to a vertical wall

tail The back end of a skateboard

transition The curved area of a ramp between the flat bottom and the vertical walls

Index